Harriet's Turn

By Jan Mark

Illustrated by Jane Cope

LONGMAN

Chapter One

It happened so quickly that she did not even realise that it had begun, and when she did understand what was happening, it was over, and everything had changed.

Three fifteen: Harriet knew that, because the church clock had just chimed, and hearing it she thought, in a few minutes Mrs Turner will tell us to pack up and line up by the gate, and she hurried to finish her drawing. The clock was not on the side of the tower that she was facing and her drawing just showed the crenellations and pinnacles at the top, the shuttered window of the belfry half-way down and the little narrow tower at the side where the spiral stairs went up.

Becca and Sarah, Lisa, Emma and Louise were round the corner, opposite the west end of the church, and they could see the clock. Harriet knew that they must be watching it because although Mrs Turner had not yet said anything they were putting away their work and dusting down their skirts where they had been sitting on the steps of the war memorial. Mrs Turner was out of sight, keeping an eye on the boys at the east end, and all around heads were bobbing up and down like gophers

leaving their holes to see if the coast was clear. Harriet put the cap on her pen, picked up her clipboard and walked across to see what the others had been doing.

Lauren Miller was standing up to draw, leaning against the headstone of James Ames and also his wife Susannah. Harriet made a wide detour around the stone to avoid having to stop and talk to Lauren. Lauren was quite new to the school. She looked all right, but Becca never took any notice of her so Harriet ignored her too. Lauren seemed to understand that this was how things were done. She was not one of those upsetting people who tried to join in games without being invited, or tried to walk home with you saying, "Let's be friends", when it wasn't their turn. Lauren knew better than to sit at the wrong table at lunch. She had tried it only once.

Becca was still drawing when Harriet looked over her shoulder. She found drawing hard work to do properly, the way Mrs Turner said they should do it.

"Look hard, have a good *long* look," Mrs Turner said, "and *then* draw."

Becca would take a good long look and then forget what she had seen before she could get it down on paper, so she drew while she was looking, wandering, wavering lines that ambled up and down the paper, with blobby holes where her pen dug in, so that her pictures always looked as if she had been joining up dots. She was using a pencil today, so the dots were less blobby, but even so her drawing looked like the work of someone who had heard about church towers but had never seen one.

"It looks like a rabbit, sitting up," Harriet said. "Look, those bits at the top, pinnacles, they're its ears, and the clock's its nose and the window is its mouth – open."

Becca giggled and the others came to look.

"And those are its knees, those buttress things," Harriet said.

"Hasn't got any eyes," Louise said.

Becca took up her pencil and pressing hard drew two large cartoon eyes with long lashes, on either side of the clock. What had been a bad drawing of a church became a funny drawing of a face. You could only call it an improvement. Becca drew long whiskers sprouting out and added two buck teeth to the window, at the top. It was probably the best thing that Becca had ever drawn.

Mrs Turner was approaching between the tombstones, followed by the rest of the class. As they went by, other people got up from among the graves and joined the end of the line. Harriet thought that they looked as if they were rising from the dead and she was very happy that it was twenty past three on a sunny March afternoon and not twenty past three in the morning.

"Everybody finished? Nothing left behind? Is that your sweater, Emma? All got your pens and pencils?" Her voice changed. She had seen the rabbit.

"Whose is this?"

They could tell at once that she was annoyed. What had been a funny picture a moment ago was suddenly a stupid waste of time, waste of paper.

"Mine, Miss," Becca said.

"I suppose you think it's clever?" Mrs Turner thought that Becca had been drawing the rabbit all afternoon.

"I never did it," Becca said.

"I suppose it was the fairies," Mrs Turner snapped.

"Hoooo! It was ghosts!" Matthew Hawkes began to gibber from behind a gravestone.

"I never," Becca said.

"You mean someone has interfered with your pictures? Who?"

"I don't know." Becca screwed her toe into the grass and swung her skirt.

"Why don't you know? Why did you leave your work lying about? What were you doing?"

Mrs Turner's questions came out in hard little chips like the green gravel on the graves.

"Did anyone see who spoiled Rebecca's drawing?"

"It was Harriet, Miss," Louise said.

Harriet did not at first take in what had been said. It was the last thing she had expected to hear.

"Harriet! Is this true? Did you touch Rebecca's picture?"

"No!" Harriet said. "Of course I didn't. She – "

"It *was* Harriet. I saw." Louise looked round at the others, Lisa, Emma and Sarah. "Wasn't it?"

They made daft sucking noises with their teeth and nodded righteously.

"She done it with Becca's pencil, Miss," Sarah volunteered.

"Well?" Mrs Turner was glaring at Harriet, furious. Furious because the afternoon was spoiled, furious because there was a row to sort out and a lie to investigate. Mrs Turner knew as well as anyone that it would never be sorted out by home time; that kind of thing never was.

Harriet had already sorted out the lie but then she was in possession of the facts and Mrs Turner was not. The facts were that Louise wanted to be Becca's best friend in place of Harriet, and thought she could make it happen by getting Becca out of trouble. Sarah wanted to keep in with Louise and would back her up whatever she said. Louise was Sarah's best friend. She could not risk annoying her. On two separate walls in the toilets Harriet had seen hearts drawn; and written in them LISA 4 JOE and

EMMA 4 JOE. Joe was Sarah's brother. If they did anything to upset Sarah it might get back to him, and now no one could say anything in Harriet's defence without calling the others liars.

Mrs Turner did not know any of this. All Mrs Turner knew was that someone was not telling the truth. The drawing had been spoiled and no one would admit to having done it.

"Well?" Mrs Turner said again.

"I didn't touch her drawing," Harriet said. "I was round the side of the tower."

"Not when I saw you."

"She did do it," Louise said, and there was a silent Mexican wave of heads as Louise, Sarah, Emma and Lisa all nodded, one after the other.

Harriet looked at Becca. If Becca had had the nerve to own up in the first place none of this would have happened but Becca could see as well as Harriet that now it was too late to say anything. If she did own up, Louise and the others would be shown up as liars. If she said nothing she was safe. The lie had solidified.

"Line up," Mrs Turner said. "Stop talking. Line up in silence by the gate – not you, Harriet."

Harriet, clutching her clipboard, stood and waited. There was a kind of silence in the line by the gate, but everyone was looking at her, standing alone beside Mrs Turner somehow asking what had happened, somehow being told that Harriet Smith had drawn a silly face on Becca's picture.

"Well?" Mrs Turner said, a third time.

"I didn't do it," Harriet said. "All I did was I said that Becca's drawing *looked* like a rabbit. It did." It was true. It sounded like the truth. Surely Mrs Turner could hear that. But Mrs Turner did not know the facts.

"Four people saw you do it," Mrs Turner said. "Do you mean to say they were all lying, that Rebecca's lying?"

"Yes," Harriet said, boldly. She could not say outright that she had watched Becca herself put in the silly eyes, the whiskers, the goofy teeth. That would sound even less convincing than just refusing to take the blame.

"Why should they make it up?" Mrs Turner really wanted to know. She did not understand how these things were done, how the wind could change and suddenly blow sand in your face.

"Perhaps one of them did it," Harriet suggested.

"But why should they all blame *you*? Have you upset them, or something?"

It doesn't work like that, Harriet wanted to say. You don't have to do anything. Alex Leacock hadn't done anything when Becca said that we didn't like her any more. We just didn't like her any more because Becca said so. We wouldn't let her sit at our table or pick her for teams. We hid her lunch box and Sarah threw her shoes in the pond. We all said we were going to drown her at swimming. We even took her money for the theatre trip and her mum had to give her some more. She never told. No one would have believed her.

'She.' Alex. In those days 'we' had included Harriet. Harriet had done what Becca said for fear of what would happen to her if she didn't. Now it had happened. She might have known that it would happen like this. She might as well have stood up for Alex. At least there would have been two of them to look out for each other.

Mrs Turner was still talking.

"Why keep denying it when everyone saw you?"

"It wasn't everyone," Harriet said. "It was Louise and Sarah and Emma and Lisa."

"They did see you, then."

"No!" Now she had almost been tricked into admitting it; had almost tricked herself. "They *said* they saw me, but I didn't do anything. I didn't have the chance."

"We'll sort this out in the morning," Mrs Turner said, wearily. Harriet knew that she wanted to sort it out now, so that there would be nothing left to worry about tomorrow, but they were already late starting the walk back to the school and buses would be waiting. Mrs Turner nodded abruptly and the line moved off into the lane that led past the pub and the council houses, straight back to school; not running, which was forbidden, but with all its legs moving very fast. People who had to catch buses managed to overtake those who lived in the village and need not worry. It looked like a complicated dance, like the one they were practising for the Maypole after Easter and, as in the one they were doing round the Maypole, legs became entangled and a fight broke out in the middle of the line.

Mrs Turner, now thoroughly angry, surged ahead to break it up and Harriet was left to tag on at the back. By this time Lisa and Emma and Sarah, who were bus people, had reached the front of the line, leaving Becca and Louise at the rear. Sticking up for your friends was one thing; missing the school bus could be a disaster. Harriet, seizing what might be an advantage, hurried to catch up.

"Are you going to own up?" she said, outright. Louise and Becca did not turn round. Harriet poked Becca on the shoulder.

"You spoiled your own drawing. Are you going to own up?"

Becca turned round and her face was quite blank.

"You did it. They all saw you."

"You're a liar," Louise said. "We don't want to walk with you."

"You're the liar," said Harriet. "Both of you. All I said was Becca's drawing *looked* like a rabbit. It was Becca that altered it."

"No I didn't. I put my clipboard down and went to talk to Sarah and when I came back you'd scribbled all over it. You tried to get me into trouble. We don't want anything to do with you any more."

Harriet fell back and walked on her own. The church clock, way behind them now, struck the eight notes of the half hour; three thirty. At three fifteen none of this had happened, it had not even begun to happen. Harriet had still been drawing. Becca had still been drawing. Harriet began to play 'if only'.

If only I had stayed where I was *three* more minutes, Mrs Turner would have got to Becca before I did. Well, Becca wouldn't have had time to start drawing eyes and whiskers, anyway. If only I'd told her to stop. If only I hadn't said anything at all. It wasn't kind to say that her picture looked like a rabbit, but it did. I wasn't *trying* to be unkind. She didn't think I was being unkind, she laughed. *She* was the one who made it into a proper rabbit. But perhaps she did think I was being unkind.

Harriet said, "Becca, I'm sorry I said that your picture – "

"I'm not talking to you," Becca said, without turning round.

"I'm apologising!" Harriet shouted.

"You got Becca into trouble," Louise said. "It's no good apologising."

"I didn't get her into trouble. She got herself into trouble," Harriet said.

"It was your fault," said Louise, and then seemed to realise that she had almost admitted that Harriet had not actually done anything. "Your fault for spoiling Becca's drawing," she amended.

They had reached the school gates, nearly five minutes late. The little ones, who were always let out first so that they would not get trampled into the tarmac, were swarming across the playground, meeting their mothers or climbing into the buses all knees and elbows, like fat spiders. Mrs Turner halted the line before it could get in among the little ones.

"Bus people go straight in, get your things and come straight out again. Leave your clipboards on the shelf by the window. Everybody else wait here."

The line broke up. Suddenly there were only ten of them left and Mrs Turner was inside, chivvying bus people. Harriet hoped that the other seven would gather round and try to find out what was going on, but they had other things to think about, gathering themselves to spring the moment the last infant got clear of the playground and Mrs Turner called them in. In any case, they were mostly boys who did not care what was going on and would not understand if they knew. If a row broke out among the boys, there was a fight and it was all over, even if they got into trouble afterwards, for fighting.

Really, Harriet thought, there was no reason why she and Becca should not fight at that moment. She would enjoy hurling herself at Becca, punching and kicking, but it would not improve matters. Girls fighting was always made to seem much worse than boys fighting.

Mrs Turner appeared at the cloakroom door and beckoned. The seven raced across the playground, cutting a swathe through the bus people who were rushing in the other direction, leaving Louise, Becca and Harriet at the gate.

"Come on, Becca," Louise said. "We're not waiting for *her*, are we?"

Harriet grabbed Becca's arm.

"Look, I thought we were friends," Harriet said.

"Friends don't scribble on other people's drawings," Louise said.

Harriet, still holding Becca's sleeve, pushed between Becca and Louise.

"You know I didn't do it. I am your friend."

"No you aren't," Becca said. She would not look at Harriet, but she did not look at Louise either.

"Then why did you ask me to your party?"

"I didn't," Becca snapped, without stopping to remember that the invitation was in writing, on a special party card.

"You did."

"Well, now I'm *un*asking you. I don't want you there. If you come I'll tell my mum to make you go home."

"She wouldn't do that," Harriet said.

"All right, you can come, but no one will talk to you. We'll all pretend you aren't there."

They would, too. Harriet knew how that was done. It was something she had done herself.

Chapter Two

Mrs Turner was back at the cloakroom door, making violent hurry-up gestures. Louise and Becca started off across the playground. Harriet followed slowly, and because she did not want it to seem that she was being left behind, she began studying her clipboard as if she had just noticed something very special about it. In fact, it was quite special, the best drawing she had done in a long while; the tower rearing up with the yew trees behind it, dark and squat, making the tower itself look even taller. Beside it the long low roofs of the chancel and side aisle reminded Harriet of the backs of two dogs standing at the heel of their owner who was upright, on two legs. She could almost see the wagging tails –

No. That was the trouble. Whatever Harriet looked at she could always see something else; a giant bat hanging upside down in the bathroom when Mum hooked her black umbrella over the shower curtain rail to drip in the bath; a crouching toad where someone had thrown a crumpled trenchcoat over a bench; an armoured division under fire, driving through long grass, when one night she switched on the light in the kitchen and five black beetles had fanned out across the door mat and run for cover; a rabbit sitting on its haunches, ears erect, when Becca had only tried to draw a church.

Becca must have thought it looked like a rabbit too, Harriet told herself, or she would not have been able to turn it into one.

"Harriet, are you going to stay out there all night?" Mrs Turner demanded, and Harriet woke up to find that she had slowed to a halt in the middle of the playground. She ran in through the cloakroom, to the classroom, where Louise and Becca were standing, looking holy and martyred, beside Mrs Turner's desk.

Mrs Turner followed her into the room. Harriet could tell that she wanted to get everything cleared up quickly and go home, for she did not live in the village and had a long drive ahead.

"Well?" Mrs Turner said. This was the fourth time.

"I didn't touch her drawing," Harriet said. "I was too busy doing mine."

"Rebecca?"

"I never," Becca said, sulkily.

"It was Harriet," Louise said, but now that Sarah, Emma and Lisa had gone for the bus it was only two against one. Mrs Turner, Harriet thought, was beginning to see things differently.

"I mean," Harriet said, "if I thought the church looked like a rabbit I'd have done it myself, on my drawing. Only I didn't. I thought it looked like dogs."

"A church looks like a church to me, not a wildlife park," Mrs Turner said. "I'm not going to stay here listening to you accuse each other. Go home now. You can tell me the truth in the morning. You've got all night to work out who did what. Put your boards away. Go on."

Becca and Louise set down their boards on top of the others and went out. Harriet saw them link arms ostentatiously in the cloakroom and cross the playground, the way that Becca usually walked with Harriet.

"You too," Mrs Turner said, stuffing books and papers into her bag.

"I wouldn't spoil someone else's work, Miss," Harriet said, laying down her clipboard carefully for fear of starting an avalanche.

"No," Mrs Turner said, "I didn't think you would, Harriet, but five people say you did. They must have a reason. Leave it till the morning."

Harriet took her bag and walked out into the playground. Of course they had a reason, especially Becca. Becca had done something silly without thinking about the consequences, and had been afraid to admit it. Louise had backed her up to get

21

her out of trouble, also without thinking of the consequences. Sarah, Emma and Lisa had their reasons too. It was all so stupid. Mrs Turner had only been annoyed when she saw Becca's rabbit, now she was angry about the lying, whoever the liar might turn out to be, and if it was not all sorted out quickly, she would go on being angry.

And that was only Mrs Turner. How would the rest of them manage? Harriet foresaw the whole business dragging on for the rest of the term, and next term too, until they all left in July – unless the wind changed again and it would suddenly be somebody else's turn.

There was no rush to be home on Thursdays because Mum took Anthony over to Gran's. Dad would be home, but he never noticed what time it was if he was gardening, and he probably would be on a day like this. Harriet looked cautiously over the wall, left and right, before she went through the gate and into the lane. To the left she could see all the way up to the junction where the road ran across. That was her way home. Becca and Louise, walking very slowly, had just reached the corner. It was possible that they simply wanted to make sure that they were still in sight when Harriet came out of the playground so that she would see them together, being friends without her, but it was also possible that they had something else in mind.

Harriet waited until they had turned the corner, into the road, and then ran very fast, back the way they had walked from the church, past the church, to the special place. It had always been special to Harriet because she had always gone there to play, since she was first allowed out on her own. Now it was special for a different reason: she never went there.

A garden wall ran along the front of the special place and although the gateway was empty the broken gate still lay in the grass, just inside. There was still a name on it, Ash Cottage. The ash referred to the tree growing on the other side of the lane, but it had another meaning for Harriet. Years ago, when she was still very small, the cottage had burned down one night and all that was left was ash, and a few charred beams and sections of brickwork. Even the ash had gone now, and in summer the weeds grew so tall around it that strangers to the village did not even know that it was there.

Today, with the weeds hardly showing yet, the blackened frame of the cottage stood out grimly against the young leaves of the willows behind it. Harriet, standing in the gateway, could almost see the building that she could not quite remember; a door in the middle, opposite the gate, a window on either side and a thatched roof that came down

right to the tops of the windows like a fringe of hair growing over someone's forehead and touching their eyebrows. That was why it had burned so quickly, because of the thatch.

Alex and Harriet had come there to play every summer. Sometimes during the spring term they would walk along after school instead of going straight home, look over the wall, look at each other and say, "Not yet." They only started going to the cottage when the weeds were high enough to hide it and it had always made Harriet feel very grown-up, having the self-control not to go there all the time, although it had been Alex who pointed out that if other people could see them there everyone would want to join in. It would not be a special place any more, but as crowded as the playground at break.

After all, they did not really play there. Instead they sat in the grassy rooms and talked. Under a flat stone they had hidden comics and favourite books and sometimes sweets. A farm cat had had her kittens in the kitchen. They called her Mrs Fattypuss and Alex had borrowed food for her from the Leacock's cat. They had been wondering about keeping the kittens, but Mrs Fattypuss seemed to know what they were thinking and took the kittens away one night, although she still came back for meals.

That had been the best summer, Harriet remembered, as she walked over the lumpy grass to the kitchen; the best summer, last summer. They had known it was the kitchen because Mrs Fattypuss had been living in the old stoneware sink that lay on the ground. Mrs Fattypuss must have stopped coming to the cottage at about the same time that Harriet and Alex also stopped coming, the time when Becca said, "We don't like Alex any more."

They had never taken Becca to the cottage, or Louise. They had never told Sarah, Emma and Lisa about it, when they all sat together in class or talked in the playground.

We were different when we were on our own, Harriet thought, sitting on the edge of Mrs Fattypuss's sink. How did Becca spoil it? I didn't have to stop liking Alex just because Becca said so. But that was exactly what had happened, and when Harriet stopped liking Alex at school, she had to stop liking her out of school as well. Becca and Louise, Sarah, Emma and Lisa had been her friends. Alex had been her special friend.

All the while they were not liking Alex, Harriet had been wondering how long it would last. Sooner or later it would be someone else's turn and she and Alex could be friends again. But Alex had gone. Her family had left the village, her dad had a new job. But at night, when she could not get to sleep, Harriet would lie and wonder if Alex had gone away because Becca had said that no one was to like her any more. One day Alex just wasn't there, and there was no time to say sorry, no chance to explain that they had not really meant it – they were just doing it. It would have been better if they *had* meant it and done nothing, like Mrs Turner and Miss Pugh. Without being told, everyone knew that Miss Pugh and Mrs Turner did not like each other very much, but they still made coffee for one another in the staffroom, and lent each other pens and scissors. Miss Pugh did not make faces and pretend to be sick when Mrs Turner spoke to her. Mrs Turner did not hide Miss Pugh's handbag or put mud in her shoes.

Why did I let it happen? Harriet thought. I wouldn't let it happen now. I'd rather have one friend like Alex than five friends like Becca and the others. But now, of course, she did not have five friends. She did not have any.

If only Alex were still here... Harriet knew, had to admit finally, that even if Alex had not gone away they could never have been friends again. And when Becca and Louise decided, some time next term perhaps, that it was somebody else's turn, would she, Harriet, want to be their friend again? She had a nasty feeling that she would because she was not like Alex. Alex had been proud. She never cried, never told tales, all the time she was not being liked.

Well, I won't either, Harriet thought. It was too late to do anything for Alex, but at least she could be like her, and when it was Harriet's turn to be Becca's friend again, she would tell Becca what to do with her friendship.

It was getting chilly in the cottage. If Harriet did not start for home soon even Dad would notice that she was late, and there really would be trouble if

Mum and Anthony arrived before she did. The church clock had been chiming regularly all the while she had been sitting there, but she had not noticed when it struck four. What had it been just now? Eight strokes; half past four. Harriet stumbled out of the cottage and ran back along the lane. It was dead straight from the church to the junction and she kept her head up all the way in case the bus with Mum and Anthony in it passed along the road ahead of her.

There was still no sign of it when she reached the corner – it was probably stuck at the roadworks for the motorway extension – but she was so occupied with looking out for it, over her shoulder, that she did not notice who was sitting on the bench by the bus stop until she came alongside it.

"Who's *that*?" said a voice. Becca.

"Dunno. I can smell her, though." Louise.

"Yeeurghhh!"

They fanned themselves vigorously to waft away the smell of Harriet. Harriet walked past without looking at them, pretending to be Alex.

"I'm going to be sick."

"Stinky Harriet."

"Ought to live in a pigsty."

"Washes her hair in manure."

She had heard it all before. Last time she had heard it, she had been saying it, too. "Stinky Alex, washes her hair in manure. Lives in a septic tank! Yeeurghhh!" Now it was her turn to listen.

Chapter Three

During the night there was rain.

If only it had rained yesterday, Harriet thought, looking at the puddles in the road. If only it had been cold and windy, proper March weather, we wouldn't have gone out to draw in the churchyard. We'd have been sitting indoors doing our collages and nothing would have happened because Becca and I were working on the same one. Harriet and Becca always worked together on things like that, projects that had to be done in pairs, always had done, always, that was, since the day last term when Becca had suddenly turned on Harriet and said, "You don't want to work with Alex Leacock. Be my partner," and they had all decided that they didn't like Alex, although no one seemed to be very sure what Alex had done. It was just Alex's turn.

"You're very quiet," Mum said at breakfast. "Anything wrong?"

Harriet wanted to tell her but knew from past experience that if you got into trouble at school, at home you got into trouble for getting into trouble. No smoke without fire, was Mum's motto. If Harriet were to explain that she had not done anything, Mum would look doubtful and say, "Well, you must have done *something*."

"Had a row with Becca," Harriet growled.

"Then you'd better make up quickly," Mum said. "You're going to her party on Saturday."

"She doesn't want me there," Harriet said.

"Why, what have you done?"

There it was, that word 'done'. Grown-ups always assumed that you must have 'done' something. It didn't work like that; ask Alex.

"We aren't friends any more, that's all. She wants to be friends with Louise."

"I thought *you* were friends with Louise. You spend enough time with her. Can't you all be friends together?"

"Oh, it's all *right*," Harriet said. "Can I leave the toast?"

"Eat it as you go," Mum said. She hated waste. Some days Dad played dustbin and ate anything left over, but he was on early turn this week and would not feel like finishing anyone's breakfast when he came home at lunch-time. Anthony, too young even for the infants, was poking soft wet cornflakes into his mouth. He did not like toast.

Harriet had to time her exit carefully so that she did not run into Becca and Louise. What on earth were they saying to each other, she wondered, seeing them far ahead of her, in the street, arms round each other's shoulders. They were both lying, they both knew they were lying, unless they had convinced themselves that what they were saying was the truth, because they had said it so many times. And never mind what they were saying, what were they thinking? What were Sarah and Emma and Lisa thinking as they sat where they always sat, on the back seat of the bus?

On the other side of the road Lauren Miller was walking, slightly ahead of Harriet. Lauren had been at school only since the beginning of term and no one knew her very well. She was not anyone's special friend or enemy, she was just there. Sooner or later, Harriet supposed, she would become part of the group around the table where she sat, but so far no one had claimed her. No one like Becca had said, "Lauren's going to sit with us," or "I want Lauren in my team," and because of that no one had said to Lauren, "Be my friend," in case no one else in the group agreed.

It occurred to Harriet, watching Lauren's lone figure in front, that if she had ever said to Lauren, "Be my friend," she would have had not only a character witness to back her up but an alibi too, very likely. If only I had, Harriet thought. If only I'd stopped to talk to her yesterday before I went to look at Becca's drawing.

It was too late now. If she overtook Lauren and

said something nice to her, Lauren would know exactly why. But without meaning to she found that she was walking a little faster, so that by the time Lauren turned down the lane that led to school, Harriet was level with her, and because they had been taught to walk safely on the right when there were no pavements, they were now both on the same side of the lane.

"Hi," Harriet said, feebly. She had meant to sound cheerful and carefree but had nervously breathed at the wrong moment.

Lauren looked at her thoughtfully and said, "What was all that about, yesterday?"

"All what?"

"All that in the churchyard, about Becca's picture."

Harriet had meant to say "Nothing," or "Mind your own business," but Lauren had asked so directly that without thinking she answered, "Becca scribbled all over her picture and said I'd done it."

"Why?" Lauren said. "To get you into trouble?"

"No, to get her *out* of trouble," Harriet said, remembering too late that in fact, to start with, Becca had only denied drawing the rabbit. It was Louise who had blamed Harriet.

"How do you know?" Lauren said.

"I just do," Harriet said, not wanting to go into

explanations about how she had put the idea into Becca's head in the first place, and then stood watching while Becca did the deed.

"Why didn't Mrs Turner believe you, then?" Lauren asked. It struck Harriet that in spite of all her questions, Lauren seemed to have worked out what had happened by herself.

"Because Sarah and Emma and Lisa and Louise all said they *saw* me do it."

"And you didn't?"

"No!"

"Really?"

"Look, what's it got to do with you?" Harriet said. "You keep your nose out of it. Nobody asked you to butt in."

Lauren shrugged and did not seem upset. She was probably used to being told to mind her own business when she asked friendly questions. That was what happened to people who did not wait their turn.

One of the buses had drawn up at the gate and stood rumbling impatiently, snorting a little, while passengers scrambled off. As soon as it was empty of village-school people it had to back up and get out of the lane, on its way to drop the big ones at the High School in town, before the other bus entered the lane from the opposite direction. There was no room for one to pass the other.

Last off the bus, because they sat at the back, were Sarah, Emma and Lisa. Harriet watched them skip down the steps and huddle together with Louise and Becca who were already in the playground, waiting. As soon as they were together, they all went into the cloakroom.

"I thought Becca was your friend," Lauren remarked. "And Louise. And the others. I thought you were *all* friends."

"I said mind your own business," Harriet cried, angrily, and accelerated away from Lauren, not into the cloakroom, that was too risky, but across the playground and round to the back, as if she had urgent business there, on the grassy patch under the trees.

She was sure that other people were watching her. That was the trouble. Everyone knew that until five past three yesterday it had been Becca–Harriet–Louise–Sarah–Emma–Lisa. Now Harriet would be missing, cast out; and everyone would know that too, and why. Mrs Turner and the other teachers, if they even noticed, might think it was because Harriet had spoiled Becca's drawing, but everyone else would know the real reason.

It was Harriet's turn.

Miss Pugh, the head teacher, was looking out of her office window.

"Where are you off to, Harriet?" she called, leaning out.

"Just going to look at the pond, Miss," Harriet said quickly, quickly altering course towards the clump of reeds in the corner by the hawthorn hedge.

"You haven't got time for that now; it's almost ten

to. Go back round to the playground."

Harriet went. This was exactly what Becca had done yesterday, lied without thinking because she was afraid of getting into trouble. But Harriet's lie had only involved the frogs in the pond. What Becca had not thought out, Harriet felt sure, was that if she said she had not spoiled her own drawing, somebody else had to have done it. If only Louise had kept her mouth shut. Mrs Turner would have got the truth out of Becca already, for Harriet was certain that if it had not been for the others, Becca would have caved in long ago.

When she went into the classroom, Louise and Becca were standing just where she had seen them yesterday, by Mrs Turner's desk, and Louise was holding Becca's clipboard; Louise, not Becca. It was Louise who was keeping things on the boil.

"Not now," Mrs Turner was saying, trying to count heads for the register. "Hurry up, Harriet. Louise, stop waving that thing under my nose. We'll deal with it after assembly. Sit down!"

They sat down, mumbling, and Harriet sat, too, but not where she usually sat. Usually she and Becca, Louise and Sarah all sat at the same table, but today Lisa and Emma were there too, and there were gaps at the table where they always sat. Harriet, desperate for a seat before Mrs Turner looked up again, sat down in Emma's vacant chair.

Joanne Clarke, eager to add to any trouble going, bounced up from the next seat, waving her arm.

"Miss! Miss! Harriet's sitting at our table, Miss."

"There's no law against that," Mrs Turner said, and her words were squeezing out between her teeth.

"But you said we had to ask you before we change places," Joanne persisted. "It's not fair – "

"Is Harriet sitting on your *lap*, Joanne?" Mrs Turner asked, looking up and taking in the rearrangements at a single glance.

"No, Miss." Joanne subsided.

"Then be quiet and stop telling tales. I'm tired of people telling tales." She was looking towards Harriet's table, where Harriet was no longer sitting. "Now, line up. We are going into assembly. If I see *anyone* causing trouble, there will be more trouble afterwards, caused by me. Do you understand?"

They understood and lined up in silence. Harriet could not help noticing that in spite of all the threats and warnings, Mrs Turner had not looked once in her direction. She remembered their conversation last night, after Becca and Louise had left.

I wouldn't spoil someone else's work.

No, I didn't think you would, Harriet.

Perhaps, in spite of all the false witness and

circumstantial evidence, Mrs Turner believed her after all. Perhaps that was why she was so angry, not because she especially liked Harriet, which she didn't, but because she hated spitefulness. Harriet had heard of big schools in cities that had security cameras. What a pity this one didn't, or at least try finger-printing. That would prove that she was innocent. She had never touched Becca's drawing.

There was trouble in assembly, in spite of what Mrs Turner had said, almost before it had started. When they all lined up to go into the hall, Harriet was standing behind Emma, so that when they got into the hall and sat down on the benches, she was still next to Emma. Emma looked at her coldly and shuffled to one side, widening the gap between them and colliding with Lisa who did the same, bumping into Sarah. Suddenly the whole line was heaving and shoving and Harriet, who had often heard about the domino effect, finally saw what it meant. If they had still been standing up, everyone would have fallen over, toppled by the person next to them. Tom Tyler, who had been absent yesterday and could not even guess about what was happening, refused to move when the domino effect reached him, so the shoving rippled back along the line, which bulged and burst, squeezing Louise and Becca into the row in front with indignant yelps.

There was a small turbulent upheaval like a mud bubble bursting in a hot spring. Mr Wright, who was just bringing in the infants, and Mrs Turner, waded through wagging heads and knees and kicking feet to find out what was going on. Mr Wright had no idea what was going on and was surprised. Mrs Turner had guessed and she was furious. She was so furious that Harriet could not imagine what she would do next, apart from bursting into flames. She could almost see it happening: Mrs Turner a roaring furnace in the middle of the hall while everyone fled for the exits and black greasy smoke spread out under the ceiling. It had not happened yet, but Mrs Turner spoke hot cinders.

"I want my class to remain behind after assembly. I have never known such dreadful behaviour. Sit down at once, Louise. Don't say anything, Emma."

"Harriet pushed me," Emma said, experimentally. The experiment was a failure.

"Harriet did *not* push you." Mrs Turner spat out one last glowing ember. "Sit!"

All through assembly, which was sad and nervous because most people did not understand what had been happening, Harriet clung on to that. Mrs Turner was not going to join in blaming her for everything that went wrong. Mrs Turner understood. It would not make any difference with

Becca and Louise and the others; they would go on hating her anyway, but at least Mrs Turner believed that she was telling the truth. That had been Louise's mistake: involving a teacher. When Becca had said that they did not like Alex any more, no one on the staff had known about it. Alex had been on her own.

At last it was over, and Mr Wright went to the piano to play music for them all to leave by. Usually he played something so lively that the infants had to be told to stop skipping, but today the heavy atmosphere had got to him and he thumped out a slow and solemn tune with lots of bass chords and a dreary trickling noise at the other end of the keyboard that reminded Harriet of thunder and overflowing gutters blocked with dead leaves in autumn.

Mrs Turner's class and Mrs Turner stayed behind in the hall, and everyone else walked out around them. Even the infants looked enormous if you were sitting down while they walked by.

"I have had enough," Mrs Turner said when the hall was empty except for them. "I have had enough of this quarrelling and tale-bearing and now fighting, and all because of a stupid, pointless incident yesterday afternoon, something so silly that I can't believe it wasn't over in a couple of minutes. Stop looking at each other. Look at me when I'm talking to you. The people involved know perfectly well who they are."

She had been glaring at everyone, eyes ranging from one end of the row to the other, rather like a security camera, Harriet thought, but now she was looking at just one end: at Becca, Louise, Sarah, Lisa, Emma and Harriet.

"In case the rest of you don't know what this is all about, I'll tell you, and you won't be able to believe it either. Yesterday afternoon, while we were drawing in the churchyard, somebody did a silly scribble on Rebecca's picture – don't say a word, Louise. I was annoyed because it was a stupid thing to do, but not half as annoyed as I am now."

You can say that again, Harriet thought. Last term they had learned about weather and the Beaufort Scale of wind speed. Mrs Turner must be at force twelve now, a hurricane.

"I thought Rebecca had done it herself, but she says she didn't. Now, Rebecca, is that true?"

Oh, go *on,* Harriet prayed. Say you did it. You can go on hating me, I don't care, just get this over with.

"Rebecca?"

"No, Miss. I never."

"All right. Harriet, did you do it?"

"No, Miss."

"I see," Mrs Turner said, and Harriet knew

precisely what she saw. The whole incident was about to achieve lift-off and go into orbit, round and round, for ever.

"Miss!"

Everyone looked round. An arm was raised at the other end of the line. Mrs Turner, surprised and wary, looked round too.

"Lauren? If you've got someting to say, it had better be worth hearing. I don't want any more false accusations."

"Yes, Miss. It was me, Miss. I spoiled Becca's drawing."

Chapter Four

"*You?*" said Mrs Turner.

"Yes, Miss. I'm sorry."

"Miss, it wasn't – "

"Louise, if you say another *word*..."

Lauren had gone mad, Harriet decided, slightly dazed. It was quite simple, she'd gone off her rocker, just like that, in the middle of assembly. You heard about it happening, of course, but usually it was grown-ups. No one knew what to do. Mrs Turner was staring at Lauren. Emma, Lisa and Sarah were staring at Lauren. Louise and Becca were staring at each other. They had all forgotten Harriet.

"But how could you?" Mrs Turner said. Usually this meant, "How could you do such a dreadful thing?" Now it meant, "But how could you have had the chance to do it?"

Lauren was quite calm. "Becca and Louise were mucking about round the war memorial, Miss, so I went and looked at Becca's picture and I thought it looked just like a rabbit, so I made it into one."

Mrs Turner did not really care about the details, Harriet could see. What she cared about was that now she would have to deal with Becca and the others for deliberately getting Harriet into trouble. Lauren might have made things better for Harriet, but not for anyone else.

But why had she done it? Harriet rapidly rewound her private video of those fatal five minutes in the churchyard. How many people had actually seen what happened, had *seen* Becca drawing the teeth and whiskers? Only Louise and Harriet herself. Lauren knew only what Harriet had told her. Why did she believe Harriet and not the others?

Harriet wondered if she ought to put up her hand and say that Lauren was innocent too, but what good would that do when Lauren herself had just said that she wasn't? She decided that now she was out of it she would stay out of it, but what was she going to say to Lauren when it was all over? She was not even sure if she felt grateful, yet.

"Why didn't you own up yesterday and save all this bother?" Mrs Turner was asking. Mrs Turner did not sound very grateful either.

"I didn't think," Lauren said. "I didn't think Becca would get into trouble. I was already lining up. I didn't know till this morning that she thought Harriet had done it."

"But she didn't *think* anything of the kind," Mrs Turner said, and now she was looking at Becca. "She *said* Harriet had done it. She said she saw her."

"I never!" Becca shouted, jumping to her feet. "It was Louise said that."

"Yes, Louise," Mrs Turner said, "you told me that you watched Harriet doing it. And you three, Emma, Lisa, Sarah."

"No *we* didn't, Miss," Lisa said. "Sarah said so, Miss. She said Harriet had done it with Becca's pencil, but *we* didn't, Miss, me and Emma. We never said nothing."

You nodded, Harriet thought, remembering the Mexican wave.

"Louise," Mrs Turner said, "why did you tell me that Harriet had done the drawing?"

"I thought – "

"You said you *saw* her. I must say," Mrs Turner went on, staring at the ceiling, not at Louise, "I must say, I did wonder why you didn't stop her."

There was silence.

"Why didn't you stop her, Louise? You must have thought it was wrong or you wouldn't have told me about it."

"I tried to, Miss."

"I get the picture. You saw what Harriet was doing and rushed to stop her, wrestled her to the ground and ripped the pencil from her grasp – yes? But it was too late. Yes?"

"Yes, Miss."

"Only it wasn't Harriet at all, was it?"

"Thought it was, Miss."

"You thought Lauren was Harriet? Stand forward, Harriet. Now, have a good look, Louise. Can you tell the difference?"

Harriet, advancing, was almost beginning to feel sorry for Louise. Harriet was tall and thin with long fair hair. Lauren was short and wide and her curly hair was almost black. If you had to choose two girls in the class who were complete opposites, you would choose Lauren and Harriet.

Louise was not looking at either of them, she was looking at the floor. Becca was also looking at the floor and Harriet saw a tear slide down her nose. Something had gone horribly wrong and Becca could not work out what, or how. Distantly Harriet heard the church clock chime eight notes: half past nine. How much longer was this going to go on, something which had taken only about half a minute to do; and the end seemed farther away than ever. What was Lauren playing at?

Mrs Turner also heard the clock.

"I think we've all wasted quite enough time," she said. "We'd better miss break to make up for it and at lunch-time we will get this sorted out once and for all. Go back to the classroom. No talking."

A discontented growl rose here and there along the line.

"Us boys too?" Matthew said. "It wasn't none of us."

"Everyone." Mrs Turner swivelled round and walked out and Harriet, at the end of the row nearest to the door, followed her, hearing the others muttering and shuffling behind her as they stood up and left the hall. By the time everyone was sitting down in the classroom not only Becca was crying but Louise too. Mrs Turner took no notice and told them all to get out the graphs they had started yesterday morning. People worked in silence, sometimes looking up cautiously when the silence was broken by a particularly wet sniff from the corner table. The sniffs increased as the morning wore on. When through the window came the sounds of the rest of the school going out to break, someone in the corner sobbed aloud. Harriet peered over the edge of her folder. Becca, Louise, Sarah, Emma and Lisa were all weeping and passing round a solitary paper handkerchief that was almost on the point of dissolving. Becca, who was the most sodden, was wiping her eyes with the end of her pony-tail.

Harriet wondered why she did not feel more pleased. It served them all right for trying to get her into trouble, but she could not enjoy it. No one was happy. The boys were outraged because they had missed break although none of this had anything to do with them, and the other girls, who had nothing to do with it either, were wondering how long it would be before they too were mysteriously involved.

It's like somebody has died, Harriet thought, and no one knows what to say. Even Mrs Turner doesn't know what to say. That's why she's making them wait till lunch-time. She's trying to work it out.

She let her eyes slide round in a northerly direction to see what Mrs Turner was doing, and on the way she caught sight of Lauren who was working away as hard as anyone on that table by the door where people sat who did not have special friends. For some reason, perhaps because she *felt* that Harriet was watching her, Lauren looked up and gave Harriet a most terrible grin. It was not a friendly grin and it made Lauren look quite evil, like a Hallowe'en mask, for the sunlight, reflecting off the cover of her folder, had turned her face green. Lauren at least was enjoying herself but, Harriet wondered, what exactly was Lauren enjoying? She had confessed to something that she had not done. Was that to get Harriet out of trouble? Harriet doubted it. She had never been very nice to Lauren, not horrible and spiteful the way she had been to Alex Leacock, just not very nice, not bothering to be anything at all, really.

Harriet had a feeling that she herself had nothing to do with it, that Lauren would have confessed whoever had been to blame for the rabbit, that in some way Lauren was getting back at Becca or Louise. But why? What had they done? If they had done anything to Lauren, Harriet would have known. Harriet would have been part of it, doing it too.

There was a gulping sound at Harriet's elbow. Now Joanne was wiping her eyes. The crying was spreading, like whooping cough. By the end of the morning, the longest morning that Harriet had ever known, half of the class was in tears.

At ten to twelve Mrs Turner, who seemed to have frozen solid at her desk, melted and stood up.

"All right," she said, "put your things away neatly. I want Rebecca and Louise, Sarah and Lisa and Emma, Lauren – and you, Harriet – to stay here. The rest of you can go out on the grass until lunch-time – but no noise. Other people are still working."

There was no noise at all. The class left so quietly that the sound of tables being set up in the hall could be heard quite clearly. The school meals van had brought something fishy for lunch. The smell rolled in as people went out.

"Come over here to my desk," Mrs Turner said, when Joanne, the last person to leave, had closed the door. They stood in a semicircle, heads bent, except for Lauren who had stopped grinning but still looked quite cheerful.

"Let's get this straight," Mrs Turner said, briskly, and Harriet knew that she had been rehearsing. "Lauren drew a silly face on Rebecca's picture. No one actually saw her do it so one of *you*," she looked at Louise, "decided to blame Harriet. Is that right?"

The Mexican wave again, very subdued. More like a Mexican hiccup.

"Harriet said she hadn't done it, but you all insisted that she had, even though you had no proof. Right? Why was that, I wonder?"

"Dunno," Sarah whispered and, like spiders in dry grass, Emma and Lisa echoed, "Dunno, Miss."

"Don't you think you owe Harriet an apology?" Mrs Turner said, and one after the other they all turned round and muttered, "Sorry, Harriet."

"It's all right," Harried mumbled each time, but it was not all right. It was all wrong. It was horrible.

"Now," Mrs Turner said, when Becca's final apology and Harriet's answer had dribbled into silence, "it turns out that the real culprit was Lauren, because she says so herself. She didn't know that Harriet had got the blame – though I can't imagine how; so Lauren owes Rebecca an apology too, I think."

"I'm sorry I spoiled your drawing, Becca, " Lauren said. Becca burst into tears all over again, real loud howling that made them all jump.

"Now what's the matter?" Mrs Turner said. "It's not the end of the world, Rebecca. All you have to do is fetch your rubber and get rid of the rabbit. It won't take long. You could have done it already. You could have done it yesterday, come to think of it."

"Oh, Miss," Becca roared, "it wasn't Lauren. I did it."

"You did it? You drew the face?"

"Yes, Miss. I'm sorry, Miss."

"But that's what I said yesterday." Mrs Turner looked bewildered. "I asked you if you had done it and you said it was Harriet."

"I was frightened you'd be cross."

"I was cross," Mrs Turner said, "but what did you think I'd *do*? How long did you think I'd be cross for? What usually happens when I catch you doing something silly?"

"You shout a bit and say 'Don't do it again', Miss," Becca said.

"Exactly. And it would all have been over in seconds. Instead of which you let me think someone else had done it. You told me it was Harriet. *That* wasn't just silly, was it? That was unkind and thoroughly dishonest."

Becca brightened, slightly. "No, Miss. I never."

"It was me," Louise said.

"So it was. Why did you do that, Louise?"

"I didn't want Becca to get into trouble."

"So you deliberately got Harriet into trouble instead. Why was that?"

Oh no, Harriet thought. Don't start, please don't start asking about that. It was my turn, like it was Alex's turn.

"I dunno," Louise said. "Didn't think."

"As far as I can see," said Mrs Turner, "thinking was the last thing that anybody did."

"It was my fault," Harriet said. "I started it – I didn't *mean* to," she added hurriedly, seeing that Mrs Turner was about to butt in. "I said Becca's drawing looked like a rabbit. She never even thought about it till I said it. I shouldn't have."

"No," Mrs Turner said. "It wasn't very kind, was it? You know how difficult Rebecca finds drawing. I should keep your opinions to yourself in future. Now, you've all had a thoroughly miserable morning which you richly deserved, and you've given the rest of us a thoroughly miserable morning which we didn't deserve at all. You'd better go and have your lunch and then run around the playground a few times. I don't want to hear anyone crying this afternoon. Lauren, I want a word with you. Off you go, Harriet."

Harriet followed the others as far as the door, but when they went along to the cloakroom to mop up with paper towels, she leaned against the wall outside and listened.

"Mmmm," Mrs Turner said, and then said nothing else.

"Yes, Miss," Lauren said, brightly.

"Lauren, why did you pretend that you were the one who spoiled Rebecca's picture?"

"So Harriet wouldn't get the blame, Miss."

"Are you and Harriet friends, then?" Mrs Turner sounded surprised.

"Oh no," Lauren said, frankly. Harriet peered round the door frame and saw that Lauren was leaning, arms folded, on Mrs Turner's desk. "But I heard them all talking while Becca was doing it. I knew it wasn't Harriet."

"Why didn't you say so then, yesterday? Think of all the grief you would have saved."

"But that would be telling tales," Lauren said, wide-eyed. "I couldn't do that."

"You mean, you'd rather have taken the blame yourself? *You* could have done that, yesterday, too."

"I just wanted Becca to own up," Lauren said. "Anyway, yesterday I hadn't worked out how to do it."

"But it was nothing to do with you, was it?"

"She did it," Lauren said. "She had to own up. She would've, too, if Louise hadn't said Harriet did it."

There was a long silence, and Harriet withdrew

in case either of them looked round and saw her.

At last Mrs Turner said, "Who *are* your friends here, Lauren?"

"What here, Miss; at school? Nobody."

"No friends at school?"

"No, Miss. I've only been here since January."

"But that's nearly three months," Mrs Turner said. "And you haven't made any friends yet?"

"Perhaps I will soon," Lauren said. "It's all right, Miss, really. It's all right. Now."

The church clock began to strike the hour. By the time the last stroke had sounded there was a queue at the door of the hall and Mr Wright was on duty, allowing five people in at a time. Some lined up at the hatch for a school meal. Others went to sit with their packed lunches. You could sit where you liked at lunch-time, so long as other people liked where you sat. Harriet took her place in the queue and wondered where she would sit today; with Becca and the others, or on her own, perhaps, or she might go and sit with Lauren, poor Lauren who had been at school for almost a whole term and had not made any friends.

When Harriet reached the door and Mr Wright waved her in, she collected her fish cakes and baked beans and looked around. She saw Becca at once, at the nearest table, not looking at her. But no one else was sitting there. Louise was at the table by the piano, with her packed lunch, Lisa was on the far side of the hall, with some of the infants. Sarah was next to Joanne, someone she never even spoke to, and Emma had gone to sit at the same table as Miss Pugh, the table that everyone avoided if they could help it, because all the teachers sat there. Harriet put her tray down on the one table left.

"What're you doing here?" Matthew Hawkes demanded, but only because she had never tried to sit with him before. She had always sat with Becca and the others, always, that was, since she had stopped sitting with Alex Leacock.

Last of all, at the very end of the line, Lauren Miller came in. She went to the serving table, loaded her tray, picked up her cutlery and then stopped, looking thoughfully round the hall, deciding exactly where she would sit.

"Do you want to sit here?" Harriet said, pulling out a chair.

"Not much," Lauren said, but she sat down anyway. "I can sit where I like, now, can't I?"

Harriet passed her the salt without being asked. In future, she knew for certain, there would be no more turns.